THIS CANDLEWICK BOOK BELONGS TO:

_____

_____

_____

_____

For Meredith

Copyright © 1996 by Kim Lewis

First U.S. paperback edition 1998

The Library of Congress has cataloged the hardcover edition as follows:

Lewis, Kim.
One summer day / Kim Lewis. —1st U.S. ed.
Summary: Little Max wants a closer look at the huge red tractor
that passes by his house, so when his friend takes him
for a walk to watch it at work, he is delighted.
ISBN 1-56402-883-6 (hardcover)
[1. Tractors—Fiction. 2. Walking—Fiction.
3. Summer—Fiction.] I. Title.
PZ7.L58723On   1996
[E]—dc20   95-20580

ISBN 0-7636-0508-5 (paperback)

2 4 6 8 10 9 7 5 3 1

Printed in Singapore

This book was typeset in Bembo Semibold.
The pictures were done in colored pencil.

Candlewick Press
2067 Massachusetts Avenue
Cambridge, Massachusetts 02140

One Summer Day

Kim Lewis

CANDLEWICK PRESS
CAMBRIDGE, MASSACHUSETTS

One day Max saw a huge red tractor
with a plow roar by.
"Go out," said Max, racing to find
his shoes and coat and hat.
He hurried back to the window and looked out.

Two boys walked along with fishing rods.

Max's friend Sara cycled past in the sun.

Max pressed his nose to the window,

but the tractor was gone.

As Max looked out, suddenly Sara looked in.

"Peekaboo!" she said.

Then Max heard a knock at the door.

"Can Max come out?"

"It's a summer day." Sara laughed,

helping Max take off his coat.

The sun was hot and

the grass smelled sweet.

Max and Sara walked down the farm road.

Max and Sara stopped to watch
the hens feeding.

One hen pecked at Max's foot.

"Shoo!" cried Max and sent the hens flapping.

Max and Sara ran through a field,
where the grass was very high.
A cow with her calf mooed loudly.
Max made a small moo back.

Max and Sara
came to the river.
"Look, the boys
are fishing."
Sara caught Max
and took off his
shoes before he
ran in to wade.

Then Max and Sara reached a gate.

Sara sat Max on top.

They heard a roar in the field

getting nearer and louder.

"Tractor!" shouted Sara and Max.

Max clung to the
gate as the tractor
loomed past.
It pulled a huge
plow that
flashed in the sun.
The field was
full of gulls.

"Let's go home," said Sara to Max.

They walked beside the freshly plowed field,

along by the river and through the grass.

Sara carried Max back up the road.

"Tractor," sighed Max and closed his eyes.

Max woke up when they reached his house.

"Good-bye, Max," said Sara. "See you soon."

Max raced inside to the window.

Sara looked in as Max looked out.

"Peekaboo!" said Max and pressed his nose to the glass.

KIM LEWIS lives on a sheep farm in northern England. She says *One Summer Day* was inspired by her neighbor's two-year-old son. "Whenever a tractor goes by, he runs to the window saying, 'Tractor, tractor, tractor.' But it's always gone by the time he climbs up on the chair to look out. This story is about a child having his heart's desire fulfilled. It is also about catching the magic moment of summer." Kim Lewis has written and illustrated several other picture books, including *Friends, My Friend Harry,* and *First Snow.*